Mountain Home

by Kate Pistone
illustrated by Paul Casale

Harcourt

Orlando   Boston   Dallas   Chicago   San Diego

Visit *The Learning Site!*

www.harcourtschool.com

Erin followed her family into the little plane. It had seats for only six passengers. She sat by herself next to the one empty seat. Erin did not feel like talking. The rest of them were chattering away as if everything were just fine.

This was the second plane they had taken today. The first one was a huge silver jet. Erin had looked out the window as the jet took off and circled over the city. She said farewell to the skyscrapers and other buildings. She said goodbye to the city that had always been her home.

The big jet had flown above the clouds. There was nothing to look at except clouds, clouds, clouds. The view from this little plane was different. Erin could see everything on the ground. What she saw were trees, trees, trees. Where was her family going?

She knew they were going to a new house. She knew the house was in the Appalachian Mountains. But what would it be like? That she didn't know.

After the plane ride came an endless car ride. "Are we there yet?" groaned Shawn. He was getting restless.

"Not yet, sweetheart," said Mom.

Erin and Stephanie frowned as they looked out at endless trees.

The only one who seemed happy about the move was her dad. Dad was so excited about moving because he was going to fulfill his dream of being a cabinetmaker. Grandpa Kline and Great-grandpa Kline had been cabinetmakers. They made cabinets, tables, chairs, benches, and other things from wood.

Dad wanted to make chairs. In fact, he had given up his restaurant job in the city so he could carry on this family tradition. Erin was sorry that her dad had made this decision. She knew she would miss her friends and her busy city life. She was convinced that there would be nothing for her to do in the mountains.

"There it is," said Mom.

"Yes, we've arrived before dark," said Dad. "You'll have time to look around and make yourselves at home."

That night Erin slept in the big room at the top of the house by herself. She was used to hearing Stephanie snoring next to her and the honks of cars and trucks going by. Now she could only hear the unfamiliar chirping of crickets. Erin missed her noisy city room.

Unable to sleep, Erin began to cry quietly. She didn't want the rest of the family to hear her wailing. Finally, she seemed to run out of tears. She turned over on her side and fell asleep.

The next day, Erin went for a walk with her mom. It didn't take long for Erin to be interested in her new surroundings. Even though Erin was stubborn about moving, she was also curious about this strange place. She had lived in an apartment building all her life. When she went for a walk in the city, there was a lot to see, but this was so different.

The noises were different here, too. Erin heard something gurgling by the side of the road. She stopped Mom to see what was making the funny noise.

It was a little river. The stream's bed was covered with rocks and pebbles. Tiny underwater plants grew between the stones. Insects with wispy legs danced on the water's surface. Dragonflies hovered close to the stream, darting from one flower to another.

"Look at that, Mom!" shouted Erin. "It's a fish!"

"Do you know what kind of fish that is?" her mom asked. Erin shook her head.

"That is a rainbow trout," Mom told her. "Maybe we can go fishing tomorrow and see if we can catch some trout."

Suddenly, the trout leaped out of the water. Its scales glistened in the summer sun. As the fish dove back into the water, it opened its mouth and took a gulp of something. Erin bent down to see.

"The trout just ate these little worms!"

"Those aren't worms, Erin. They're baby insects," replied Mom. "They're probably dragonfly larvae."

"Trout eat baby insects? That sounds like a dreadful meal! Why do they eat insects?"

"It's only natural for the trout, honey. That's just what they eat," answered Mom.

Erin and Mom continued to walk deeper into the woods. "What's that up ahead?" asked Erin. "It looks like something blocking the stream." She ran to look at the mysterious object. Her eyes widened in amazement as she realized what she had found.

"Could this be a beaver dam, Mom? It's made of sticks!" Just then, they heard a high shrill scream. Erin was scared, but Mom kept her wits about her.

"Erin, keep still," Mom whispered.

A huge bird dove down from the sky. Erin thought it would hit the water head first. Before she knew it, the bird stuck out its claws and caught a fish. Then it turned and flew away over the trees. The fish was clutched tightly in the bird's claws.

Erin let out a sigh of relief. "That was kind of scary!" she exclaimed. "I was brave, wasn't I, Mom?"

"You were very brave, Erin," answered Mom. "That big bird was an osprey."

Labels in image: Cottage, Stream, Osprey, Dam, Trout, Forest

"We've had a very exciting walk!" Erin said. "It's made me thirsty. Can we go home and make some lemonade?"

When they got home, Erin decided to draw a map of the places she had seen on her walk. She found her markers in one of her unpacked boxes and began drawing. She started with their house, then added the forest, the stream, the beaver dam, and the osprey.

As Erin drew, she began to think about what she was drawing. The living things in the environment around her house all depended on each other. The insects depended on the water so that they could lay their eggs. The rainbow trout depended on the insects for food. The osprey depended on the rainbow trout for food, and the beavers depended on the trees for branches to build their dam. Erin put down her crayons and ran to find Dad.

"Dad!" she called. "I need to tell you something important."

"What is it, honey?" Dad replied.

"If you cut down all these trees and turn them into chairs, the beavers will have no way to build a dam! If that happens, the ospreys won't be able to catch fish!"

"What do you mean, sweetheart?" said Dad.

"What I mean is, Mom and I saw all of these wonderful creatures on our walk today. They all depend on the trees. If you cut them all down, none of the animals will survive."

"Thanks for your good advice, Erin," replied Dad. "You're right. I know how the environment works. I'm not going to cut down all of the trees. I will change the environment a little, but I'll be careful not to change it too much. Part of my job is making sure that the environment stays balanced."

Erin was glad that she had spoken with Dad. She was glad that there would be food and shelter for all the creatures in the forest.

Erin realized that her new mountain home was just as exciting as her old city home, but in a different way. That night, in her big, new room, she listened happily to the lullaby of the crickets as she drifted off to sleep.